This book
belongs to...

Grace
Stelling

SWEET
DREAMS
STORIES

A Collection of Bedtime Tales

This is a Parragon Book
This edition published in 2002
Parragon, Queen Street House,
4 Queen Street, Bath BA1 1HE, UK

Copyright © Parragon 2001

ISBN 0-75258-578-9

Printed in China

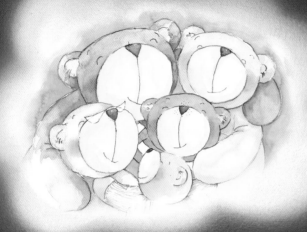

SWEET DREAMS
STORIES

A Collection of Bedtime Tales

p

CONTENTS

On my
own

Written by Jillian Harker
Illustrated by Louise Gardner

Deep in the jungle, where only wild things go, Mungo's mum was teaching him what a young monkey needs to know.

"Some things just aren't safe to try alone," she said.

"Why not?" said Mungo crossly. "I'm big enough to do things –

on my own!"

"Now Mungo,"

said Mum, "listen carefully, please.
We're going to go through these
trees. Stay close to me, and hold
my hand. Did you hear what I said?

Do you understand?"

"It's okay, Mum. I won't slip or fall. I can swing across there with no trouble at all," said Mungo. "I'm big enough to do it—
on my own!"
And off he swung!

14

"Hissss,"
hissed Snake,
in a snake sort
of wail.

"That pesky Mungo
pulled my tail!"

16

And did Mungo hear poor old Snake groan?

No!
Mungo just laughed.
"I told you I could do it
on my own."

"Now, we're going to cross the river using these stones," said Mum. "But, Mungo, I'd rather you didn't do this alone."

"But Mum," said Mungo, and he ran on without stopping, "I'm really good at jumping and hopping. I'm big enough to do it–

on my own!"

And off he sprang!

"That Mungo trampled on my nose!" said Croc.

"Next time, I'll nibble off his toes!"

And did Mungo hear poor old Croc groan?

No! Mungo just smiled. "I told you I could do it on my own."

"Mungo," said Mum, with a serious look on her face, "the jungle can be a dangerous place. There are all sorts of corners for creatures to hide, so, from here on, make sure that you stay by my side."

"Oh, Mum," said Mungo, "I don't need to wait for you. I can easily find my own way through. I'm big enough to do it—
on my own!"

Lion rubbed the lump on his nose.

"Ouch!

That Mungo's so careless!" he said.

And did Mungo hear poor old Lion groan?
No! Mungo just grinned. "I told you I could do it
on my own."

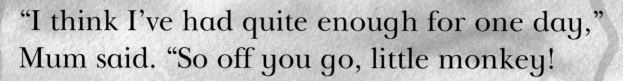

"I think I've had quite enough for one day,"
Mum said. "So off you go, little monkey!

Now it really is time for bed!"

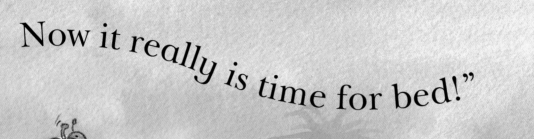

It was Mungo's turn to let out a groan.

"I don't want to go to bed –
on my own!"

"Don't worry," said Mum. "Come on,
kiss me goodnight, and I promise I'll
hold you and cuddle you tight."

Lion roared, "Is that Mungo still awake?" "Yes!" snapped Crocodile.

"Let's help him go to sleep," hissed Snake.

And into the velvety, starry sky drifted
the sounds of a jungle lullaby.

35

the end

If you hold my hand

Written by Jillian Harker

Illustrated by Andy Everitt-Stewart

Oakey's mum opened the front door. "Come on, Oakey. Let's go outside and explore."

ROSE
OTTAGE

But Oakey wasn't really sure. He was only small, and the world looked big and scary.

"Only if you promise to hold my hand," said Oakey.

So Oakey's mum led him down the long lane. Oakey wished he was back at home again!

"This looks like a great place to play. Shall we take a look? What do you say?" asked Oakey's mum.

"Only if you hold my hand," said Oakey.

And Oakey did it!

"Look at me! I can do it!" he cried.

"This slide looks fun. Would you like to try?" asked Oakey's mum.

Oakey looked at the ladder. It **stretched** right up to the sky.

"I'm only small," said Oakey. "I don't know if I can climb that high –
unless you hold my hand."

And Oakey did it!

"Wheee! Did you see me?" he cried.

49

"We'll take a short cut through the wood," said Oakey's mum.

"I'm not sure if we should," said Oakey. "It looks dark in there. Well, I suppose we could – *will you hold my hand?*"

And Oakey did it!

"Boo! I scared you!" he cried.

Deep in the wood,
Oakey found a
stream, shaded by
beautiful tall trees.

"Stepping stones, look!"
said Oakey's mum.
"Do you think you could jump

across these?"

"Maybe," said
Oakey. "I just need you
to hold my hand, please."

And Oakey did it!

two...

One...

three...   four...

"Your turn now, Mum," cried Oakey,
holding out his hand.

Beyond the wood, Oakey and his mum
ran up the hill, and all the way
down to the sea.

"Come on, Oakey," called his mum.

"Would you like to paddle in the sea with me?"

59

But the sea looked big, and he was only small.

Suddenly, Oakey
knew that didn't
matter at all.
He turned to
his mum and

smiled...

"I can do **anything** if you hold my hand," he said.

the end

Just
as well, really!

Written by Jillian Harker
Illustrated by Julie Nicholson

Rumpus liked water.

He liked the
drippiness and
droppiness,

the splashiness
and sloppiness
of it!

He liked it so much that, whenever there
was water around...

...Rumpus somehow always managed to –

But Mum loved Rumpus, so

every time, she simply sighed—and she mopped up the mess.

Rumpus loved
mud.

He loved the way
you could
plodge
in it,

splodge
in it,

slide
in it and
glide
in it!

He loved it so much that, whenever there was mud around…

...Rumpus somehow always managed to–

But Dad loved Rumpus, so

every time, he simply sighed – and
he sponged off the splatters.

Rumpus enjoyed paint.

He liked to
s**platter**
and
dash it,

to spread
and
s**plash**
it!

He enjoyed it so much that,
whenever there was paint around...

But Rumpus' brother loved him, so

every time, he simply sighed—and he cleaned himself up.

Rumpus liked to find out how things worked.

He loved the prodding and probing,

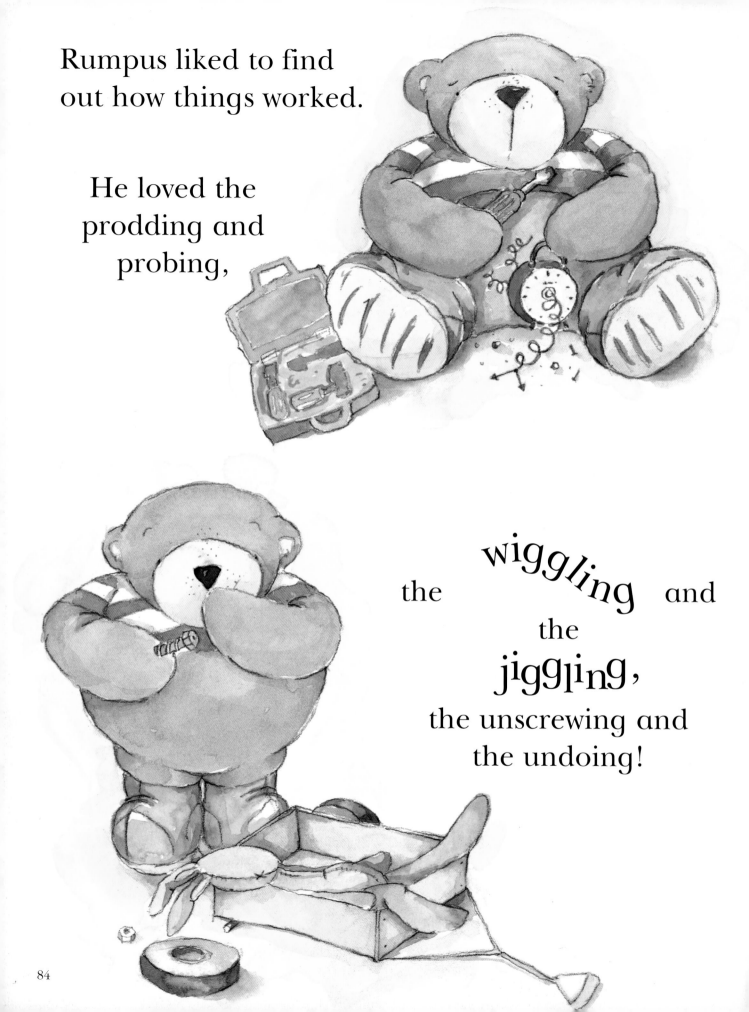

the **wiggling** and the **jiggling**, the unscrewing and the undoing!

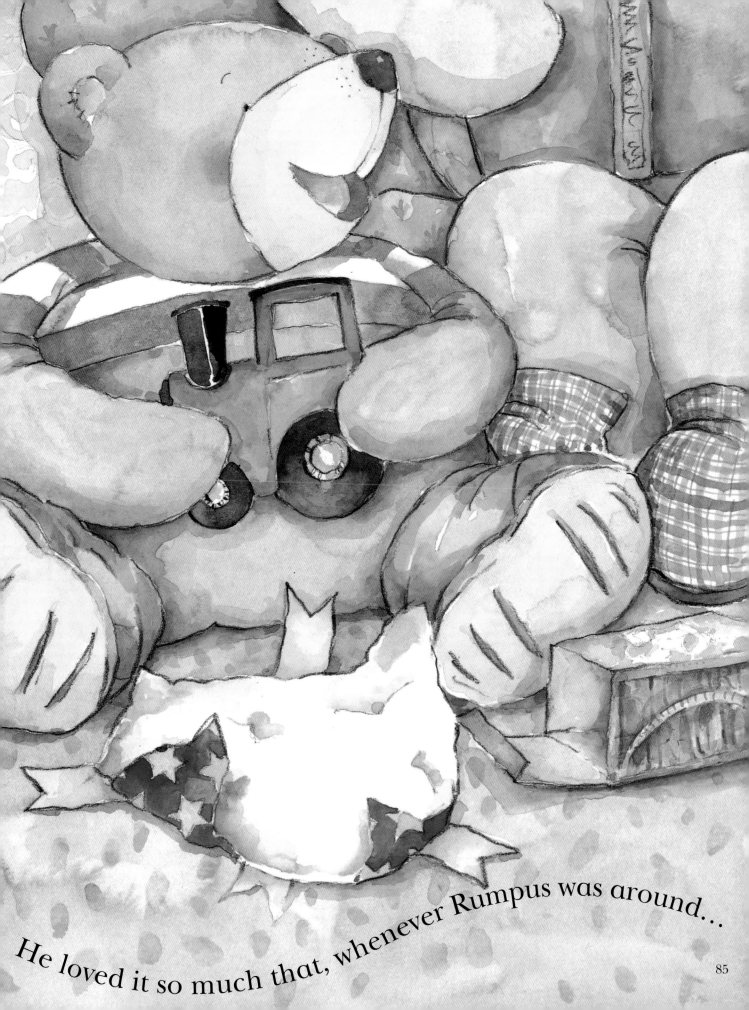

He loved it so much that, whenever Rumpus was around...

...things didn't work for long!

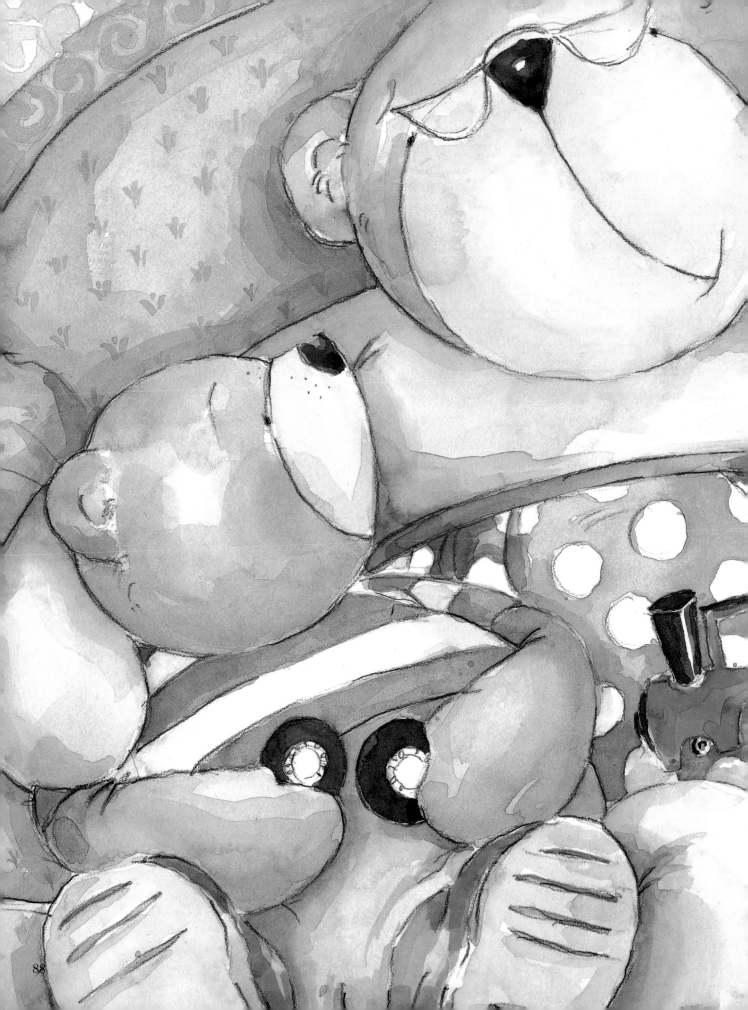

But Granny loved Rumpus,
so she simply sighed—and
she tidied away the clutter.

Rumpus loved his
mum, dad…

brother and granny…

90

Rumpus' mum, dad, brother and granny loved Rumpus…

…just as well, really!

the end

Lost
and
alone

Written by Jillian Harker
Illustrated by Louise Gardner

Deep in the jungle, Mungo was trying
to slip off through the trees.

"Mungo, tell me where you're going,
please," called Mum.
"What are you planning to do today?"

"I'm just going to play," smiled Mungo.

"Okay," said Mum.
"But no monkey business!"

Elephant was enjoying a peaceful drink,
when Mungo crept up and yelled,
"Hi, Elephant!
Want to play?"
Then he added, "I know a good game."

"Funny faces!" said Mungo.
"What do you say?"
"I'm not sure," said Elephant.
"I don't know how to play."

"Easy" said Mungo. "All you have to do, is pull a funny face. Look, I'll show you."

And he took hold of Elephant's trunk.

Mungo wound Elephant's trunk round and round
and slipped the end through.
He pulled it into a knot.

"Wow, Elephant!" he giggled.
"What a funny face you've got!"

"Hey!" gurgled Elephant. "How do I get out of this?"

But Mungo was gone!

Down by the river bank,
Crocodile was trying to nap,
when Mungo jumped out of the trees,
and gave his nose a tap.

"Want to play?" Mungo asked.
"I know a good game."
"Really?" said Crocodile,
suspiciously.
"What's its name?"

"Funny Faces," said Mungo.
"What do you say?"
"I'm not sure," said Crocodile.
"I don't know how to play."

"Easy," said Mungo. "All you have to do, is pull a funny face. Look, I'll show you."

And he took hold of Crocodile's jaws.

Mungo pulled on one jaw, and pushed on the other.
Then he jammed them both together.

"Hey, Croc!" he giggled.
"That's a really funny face!"
"Help!" choked Crocodile. "How do I get out of this?"

But Mungo was gone!

Lion was trying to
have a laze in the sun
when Mungo swung down and asked,
"Want some fun?" Then he
added, "Come on. I know a good game."
"Yeah?" said Lion, suspiciously.
"What's its name?"

"Funny Faces,
said Mungo.
"**What do
you say?**"
"I'm not sure," said Lion.
"I don't know how to play."

"**Easy,**" said Mungo.
"All you have to do, is pull a
funny face. Look, I'll show you."

And he took hold of
Lion's bottom lip.

Mungo pulled the lip up over Lion's nose.
"You see," he said, "that's the way it goes."

Then he ran off, smiling, through the trees.
"Forget what Mum said," thought Mungo.
"I'll do as I please."
He swung through the branches, but, after a while,
Mungo's face lost its smile.

"I don't know where I am!" he wailed.

"That's a funny face," said Elephant.
"He wins the game for sure."

"You're right," laughed Lion.
"Come on, Mungo, give us more."

"It's not a game," howled Mungo.
"I'm lost and alone.
I want my Mum! How do I get out of here?
This isn't any fun!"

"Well, shall we help him?" Lion roared.
"What do you think?"

"I'm not sure," said Elephant.
"He did disturb my drink."

"And he woke me up," Crocodile complained,
"which really wasn't fun."

"He wrecked my rest, too," Lion said.
"You're not the only one."

"If we agree to help, Mungo,"
he animals all said. "Then no more funny faces.
Can you get that into your head?"

Mungo looked much happier than he'd
done in quite a while.
"No more tricks!" Mungo promised,
and he thanked each of the three.
"Being lost and alone
wasn't any fun for me!"

A
goodnight
kiss

Written by Jillian Harker
Illustrated by Andy Everitt-Stewart

"It's bedtime now,
Oakey," said Mum.

122

Oakey curled up in the chair.
His ears began to droop and he muttered,
"Oh, that's not fair!"

"Have a drink first," smiled Mum, "then you must go."
"Five minutes more!" begged Oakey.
Mum answered, "No!"

Oakey's ears drooped and off he went.
But he was **back in a flash!**

125

"Where's your drink?" asked Mum.
"You haven't been very long.
You look scared, Oakey.
Is there something wrong?"

"There's a monster
in the kitchen,
with long, white shaggy hair,
lurking in the corner,
behind the rocking chair,"
said Oakey.

Mum laughed.
"Oh, Oakey, you've made
a mistake.
That's no monster. It's a mop.'
And she gave the mop a shake

128

Oakey's ears drooped
and off he went.
But he was
back in a flash!

"What's the matter?"
asked Mum.

"There's a ghost
in the hallway, hovering around.
Look, there it is floating
just above the ground,"
he wailed.

"Oh, Oakey, you've made a mistake.
That's no ghost.
It's just an old coat, hanging on the hook.
Coats don't float!" laughed Mum.

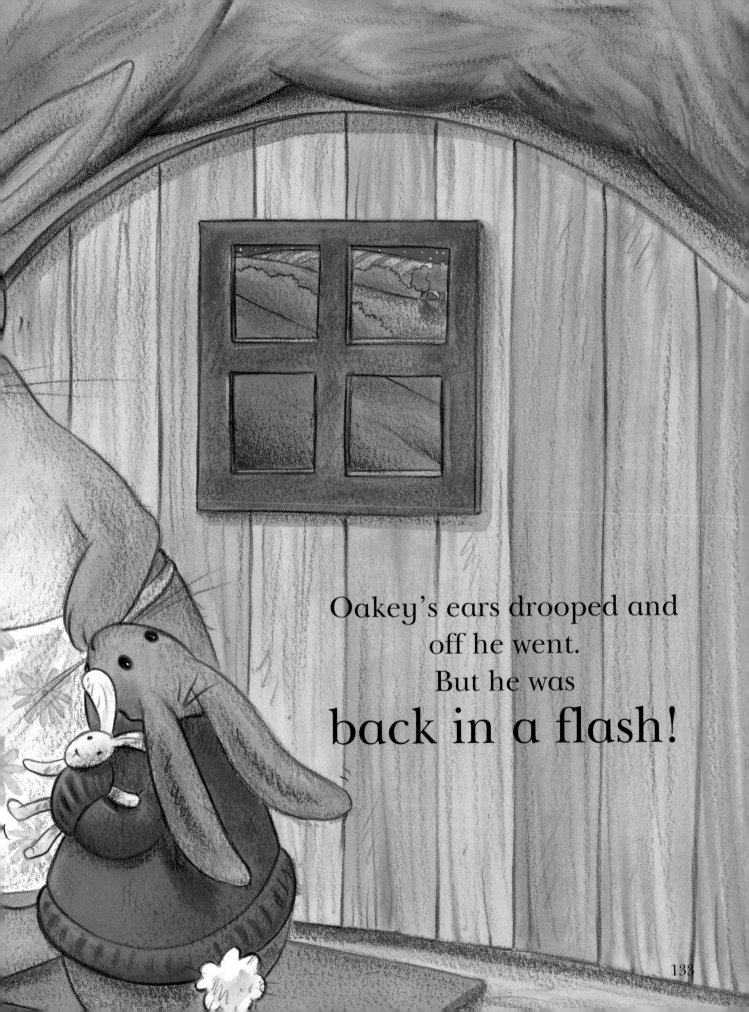

Oakey's ears drooped and
off he went.
But he was
back in a flash!

"Why aren't you in bed, Oakey?"
asked Mum.

"There's a
great big lump
beneath the sheets.
It's waiting to get me.
I'm scared it's going to pounce.
Please come and see,"
sniffed Oakey.

"Oh, Oakey, you've made a mistake.
The only thing underneath the sheets,
is your old teddy bear," smiled Mum.

136

Oakey's ears drooped
and he got into bed.
But he didn't
close his eyes.

"Why aren't you asleep?"
asked Mum.

"There are
huge creepy crawlies
underneath my bed.
And I can't get the thought of them
out of my head,"
complained Oakey.

"They're just your slippers, Oakey, so there's no need to hide. They won't be creeping anywhere without your feet inside," grinned Mum. "That's it now, Oakey. Time to say goodnight."

Mum turned and left the room, switching off the light.

141

And then Oakey saw it,
standing by the door.
The monster!

It moved across the floor and
walked straight towards him,
with its arms stretched out.
Oakey's mouth opened,
but he found he couldn't shout.

The monster leaned over him and Oakey closed his eyes. What happened next gave Oakey an enormous surprise. The monster picked him up and cuddled him tight. Monsters just don't do that.

This couldn't be right!

Then Mum's voice whispered
"Don't worry, it's just me.
When I said 'Goodnight' just now,
I forgot to give you this."

Then Monster Mum gave Oakey
a goodnight kiss!

147

the end

Kiss
it better

Written by Jillian Harker

Illustrated by Julie Nicholson

Rumpus was romping around the living room. He cartwheeled across the carpet.

He turned a somersault on the sofa.

"Be careful!"

called Mum.

Too late! Rumpus slipped from the sofa, crumpled onto the carpet and banged his head on the floor.

153

"Come here and I'll
kiss it better,"
said Mum.

154

She hugged Rumpus and planted a kiss
on his forehead.

"Now, go and find something
less rowdy to do," she said.

Rumpus rushed out into the garden
and began to ride his bike.
Round and round, he raced.

"Watch out!"
called Mum.

Too late!

Rumpus crashed into the corner of the wheelbarrow…

and tumbled to the
ground and grazed his
knee.
"My leg hurts!"
he wailed.

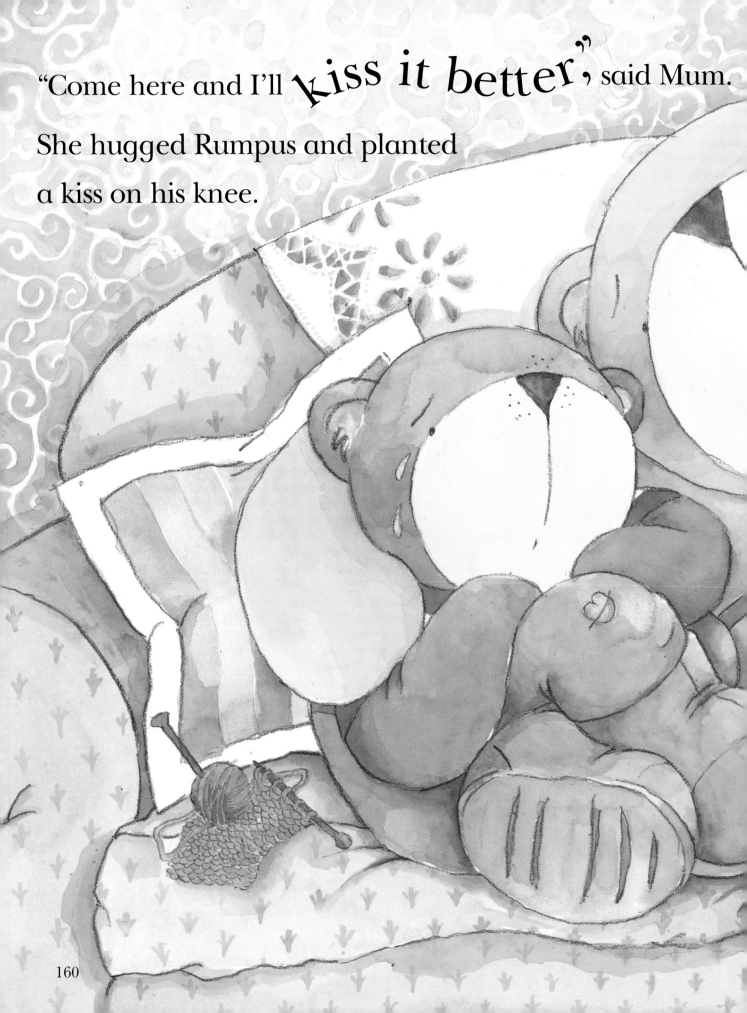

"Come here and I'll *kiss it better*," said Mum.

She hugged Rumpus and planted
a kiss on his knee.

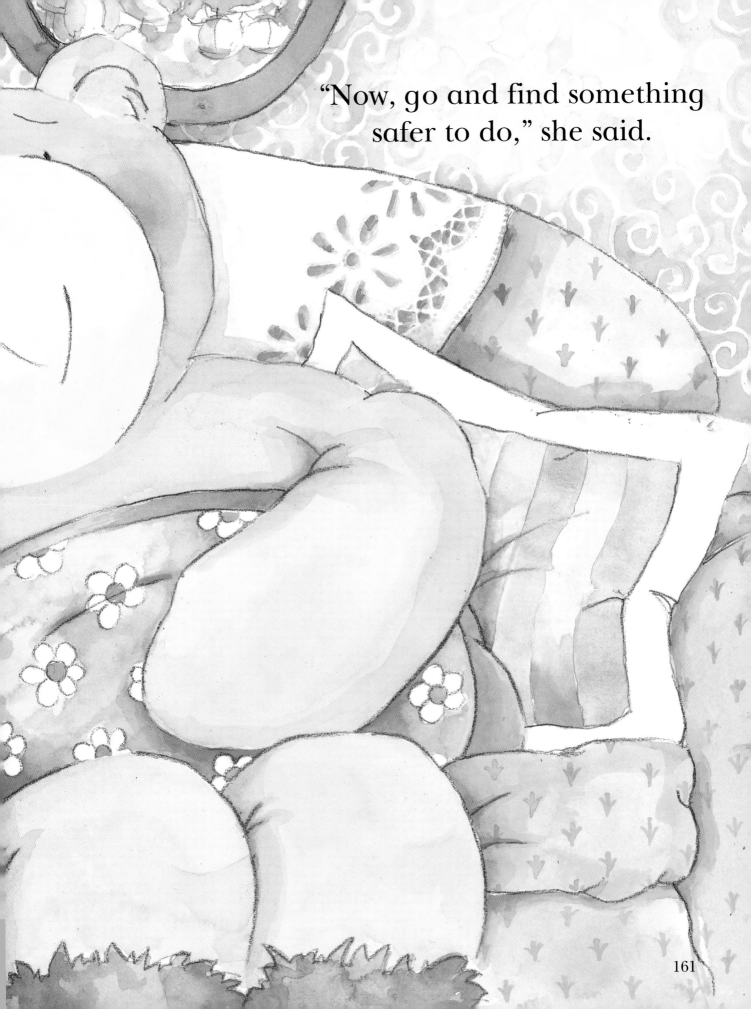

"Now, go and find something
safer to do," she said.

Rumpus ran up the grassy slope.

Then he rolled down.

"Roly poly, down the hill," he sang.

"Look where you're going!"
called Mum.

Too late!

Rumpus rolled right into the
rose bush.
The thorns scratched him all
along his arm.

"My arm's sore!"
cried Rumpus.

"Come here and I'll **kiss it better**," said Mum and she planted kisses all up his arm.

"Now, try and keep
out of trouble,"
she said.

Mum went into the kitchen.
"I need a break,"
she thought.

168

She made a cup of tea.
She cut herself a slice of cake.
Then, she sat down for five minutes.

Just as she picked up her cup,
Rumpus zoomed into the kitchen...
on his skateboard.

"Rumpus!" said Mum.
"Can't you find something more sensible to do?"

Mum moved into the living room.
"I need a rest," she thought. She sat down
on the sofa, and picked up the paper.

"Boom!
Boom!
Boom!"

In marched Rumpus,
banging on his drum.
Mum sighed a loud sigh.

173

"Is anything wrong?" asked Rumpus.

"I've got a headache!" said Mum.

174

"Never mind," smiled Rumpus, throwing his arms round her. "I'll soon *kiss it better*."

the end